GREAT HORNBILL: Found in parts of Africa and Asia, this large, ponderous-looking bird has a prominent ridge, or horn, on its large bill. It hops about in a clownish manner while catching its food in mid-air.

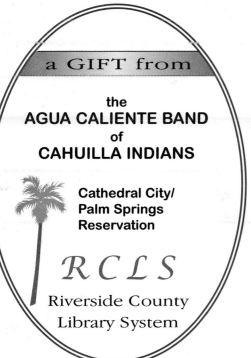

GROUSE: This heavy-bodied, chicken-like bird roams through grass and forests of Europe, Asia, and North America looking for seeds and insects to eat. A favorite with hunters, it makes a whirring sound and is capable of great speed and agility.

when
Agnes
caws

written by
CANDACE FLEMING

illustrated by
GISELLE POTTER

AN ANNE SCHWARTZ BOOK
ATHENEUM BOOKS FOR YOUNG READERS

*For Scott and Michael, whose outrageously silly
birdcalls were pure inspiration!*
—C. F.

For Kieran
—G. P.

Atheneum Books for Young Readers
An imprint of Simon & Schuster Children's Publishing Division
1230 Avenue of the Americas
New York, New York 10020

Text copyright © 1999 by Candace Fleming
Illustrations copyright © 1999 by Giselle Potter

Book design by Angela Carlino
The text of this book is set in Lomba.
The illustrations are rendered in ink.

First Edition
Printed in Hong Kong

10 9 8 7 6 5 4 3 2

Library of Congress Cataloging-in-Publication Data
Fleming, Candace.
When Agnes caws / by Candace Fleming ; illustrated by
Giselle Potter. —1st ed.
p. cm.
"An Anne Schwartz book."
Summary: When eight-year-old Agnes Peregrine, an
accomplished birdcaller, travels with her mother to the
Himalayas in search of the elusive pink-headed duck, she
encounters a dastardly foe.
ISBN 0-689-81471-2
[1. Birdsongs—Fiction. 2. Birds—Fiction. 3. Humorous stories.]
I. Potter, Giselle, ill. II. Title.
PZ7.F59936Wh   1999
[E]—dc21   97-32921

FIRST
EDITION

Agnes Peregrine, daughter of the well-known ornithologist, Professor Octavia Peregrine, was a real birdbrain.

At the age of three, Agnes could do the courtship dance of the blue-footed booby.

At the age of five, she could imitate the flight of the yellow-bellied sapsucker.

But it wasn't until Agnes was eight that her greatest skill was revealed. Two days into a bird-watching trip to Borneo, a shriek pierced the jungle air.

"*Cawaak! Caweek! Eek! Eek! Eek!*"

Agnes's mother, Professor Peregrine, whipped out her binoculars. "Did you hear that?" she whispered. "It was the call of the golden-fronted leafbird."

"You mean this?" asked Agnes. "Cawaak! Caweek! Eek! Eek! Eek!"

Out of thin air, a flock of leafbirds flitted to the ground.

"Why, Agnes," declared her mother. "You have a true talent for birdcalling."

"I do!" whooped Agnes. "I really do!"

Agnes practiced her skill wherever she went.

On the African savanna she called the great hornbill. "Pee-up! Pee-up! Pee-pee-oh!"

In the rain forests of New Guinea she called the sulfur-crested cockatoo. "Chac-ca-cha-ca! Wick! Wick! Wick!"

And deep in the swampy Everglades she called the sharp-beaked snake bird. "Chup-lup! Chup-lup! Chup-lup!"

In New York City's Central Park she called the ruby-throated hummingbird. "Hmmmmmmmm!"

Agnes's talent made bird-watching easy. It also made news. Reporters, photographers, nature lovers, all went atwitter over the little girl. But the greatest honor came from the World Bird Society.

Its members voted to send the Peregrines in search of the rarest, most elusive bird of all—the pink-headed duck!

"Spotting that duck will be a challenge," Professor Peregrine explained. "It hasn't been seen in decades."

"Bet I can call it," said Agnes. "And I bet it will come."

"There's only one problem," admitted her mother. "No one knows what the pink-headed duck sounds like."

"Then I better get quacking," replied Agnes. And she warbled a round of duck calls.

Meanwhile, on the other side of the Atlantic, Colonel Edwin Pittsnap, avid bird collector, sat in his country manor house. All around him were the spoils of his many hunts. Grouse were mounted above the mantel. Pheasants under glass served as end tables. Every nook and cranny was crammed with dead birds.

And Pittsnap craved still more.

Now the colonel opened his newspaper and read about the Peregrines. "A pink-headed duck!" he hissed. "I've so longed to get my hands on one of those. But how? HOW?"

A crooked idea came to him.

"It's deliciously crafty," he cackled. "It's superbly cunning! It's sure to work!" And rubbing his hands over his dastardly plan, he hurried to pack.

The Peregrines also packed. And then they set off on their trek.

By ship.

By train.

By yak.

Until, at last, they reached the far-off slopes of the Himalayan Mountains, home of the rare pink-headed duck.

As soon as they'd pitched camp, Agnes started calling. Little did she know that cleverly hidden on a nearby slope, Colonel Pittsnap watched and waited. . . .

Day after disappointing day, Agnes cawed. Dozens of birds answered, but, alas, not one pink-headed duck.

"This is for the birds," Agnes hollered, fed up, and she kicked a sharp rock. "Ouch-ow! Ouch-ow! Oh drat!" she cried, rubbing her stubbed foot.

"*Ouch-ow! Ouch-ow! Clack! Clack!*"

The Peregrines looked up. Overhead flew the rare, the elusive—

pink-headed duck!

The little duck flapped to the ground.

"Wow," whispered mother and daughter.

"Now!" whispered Colonel Pittsnap. He reached for his net.

SWOOSH!

"*Ouch-ow,*" cried the duck.

"At last!" crowed Colonel Pittsnap. He darted away with his
catch.

The Peregrines were stunned. "Where'd he come from?" Agnes asked.

"No idea," said her mother.

"Hey!" Agnes yelled. "That's my duck!" And she charged after him.

"Agnes!" cried her mother. She charged after her daughter.

It wasn't long before Agnes found herself on a distant slope, closing in on Colonel Pittsnap. Boldly, she stepped into view. "Hand over that duck!" she demanded.

Colonel Pittsnap jumped. He smiled a fake smile. "My, what a surprise," he said in an oily voice. "I came to capture the pink-headed duck, and by chance caught the golden-throated birdcaller, too."

The colonel threw back his head and laughed wickedly. Then, staring hard at Agnes, he demanded, "Call some birds for my collection."

"I won't!" cried Agnes. "You can't make me."

Colonel Pittsnap's nostrils flared. "I have ways of making you squawk," he hissed. And he took a step toward the small girl.

By the look on his face, Agnes knew he meant business. There was only one thing to do.

"Caw! Squawk! Cheep! Chirp! Chacalaca-wooo! Kip-whip! Hoot! Quack! Cock-a-doodle-doo! Twitter-tee! Chup-chup-chup! Wick-wick-wick! Caweek! Gobble-gobble! Ack-ack! Pee-pee-oh! Pee-wee!" she cried.

In a wing's beat, and from all corners of the world, the birds replied—hundreds and hundreds of them. They rose from their roosts. They soared through the sky. And with a cacophony of angry cries, they surrounded the colonel.

"You little fool," screamed Pittsnap. "You called too many!" He swiped at the feathered air, but the birds refused to leave. Grouse buzzed him. Pheasants bombarded him. Around and around, the birds swirled, nipping, poking, pecking, scolding.

Around and around jumped Colonel Pittsnap, weaving, swatting, crouching, dodging. And watching it all was Agnes.

Suddenly, into the fray came Professor Peregrine. "Agnes!" she cried. "What happened?"

"He asked me to call the birds," answered Agnes. "So I did."

At that moment, the birdpecked colonel let out a tremendous "Aaaagh!" and made a mad dash down the mountain. The birds swarmed after him.

Professor Peregrine turned to Agnes. "Well done," she praised.

"Thanks, Ma," said Agnes, "but the birds really did it."

Gently they untangled the pink-headed duck from the net.

"*Clack!*" said the duck, ruffling its feathers.

"Clack," said Agnes.

Then, paddling on webbed feet to reach flying speed, the pink-headed duck took to the air and winged its way over the horizon.

"Wow,"
said Agnes.

RUBY-THROATED HUMMINGBIRD:
This tiny bird's wings beat so fast that they
sound like the hum of a bee. Otherwise
soundless, hummingbirds exist around North
America, though the ruby-throated variety can
be found only in the East.

SULFUR-CRESTED COCKATOO: Also
known as the "cage bird," this bird of Australia
and New Guinea is loud and boisterous, and can
be taught to talk.

SNAKE BIRD: Common to the Florida
Everglades, this bird dives beneath the open
waters of the marsh, where it uses its long, sharp
beak to spear fish.

AMAZING ANIMALS OF THE WORLD

Albatros

CHAPTER I.

Are you sitting comfortably? Do you have a good spot? Great. Because what you're about to witness is an incredible psychedelic show, a good old journey to the end of the rainbow. Wheee! Get ready for a colorful ride, the likes of which not even the biggest amusement parks all over the world can offer. You'll get dizzy twice over and then some. I hope there's no one in the audience with a weak stomach! Gird up your loins for the most colorful among the colorful, for wonders of Mother Nature all artists wish they could imitate. To get the colors right, you'd first have to use up all your markers and crayons and then send your mom to get more from the store. Please, give a warm welcome to the most multi-colored animals in the world!

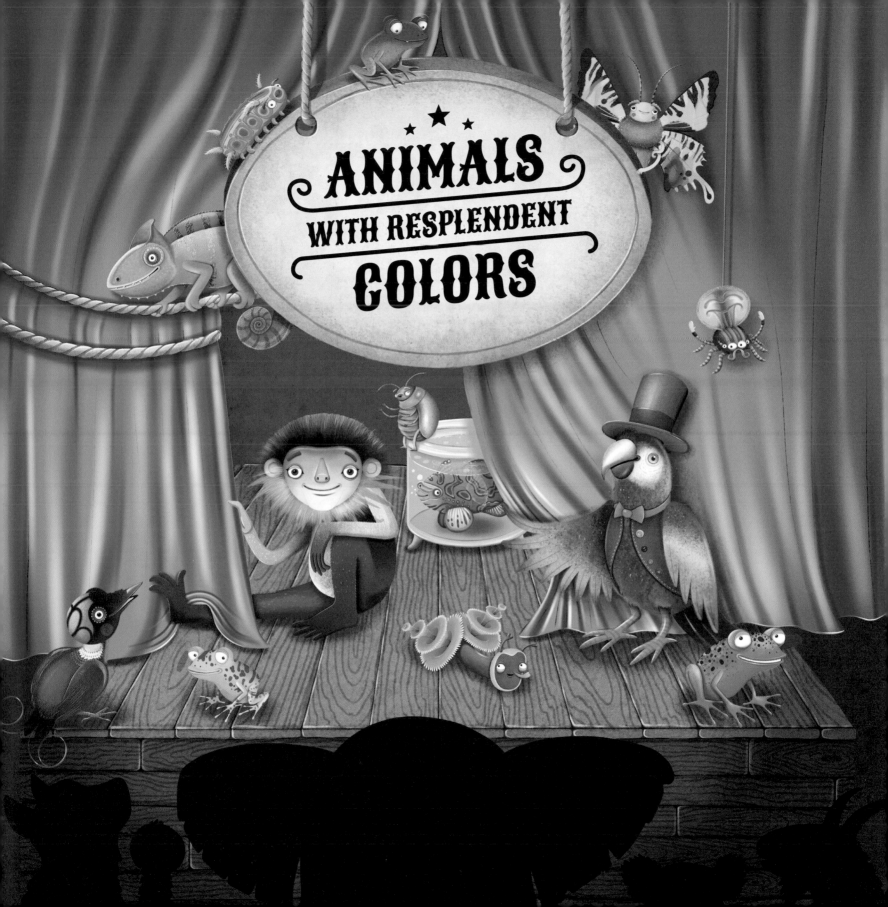

ANIMALS
WITH RESPLENDENT
COLORS

CHRISTMAS TREE WORM

The incredible beauty of coral reefs in tropical oceans attracts many divers. In that magical undersea garden, some of them stumble across a tiny live Christmas tree. Just imagine! This "tree" is, in fact, a worm—a distant cousin of the earthworm we know so well. Unlike our earthworm, however, the Christmas tree worm builds a tube in which it hides most of its body; only its bright-colored, tree-like tentacles remain exposed. As for the color of these "branches," choose one and you shall have it—deep blue, rich yellow, orange, pink with white bordering, you name it! The Christmas tree worm uses this arrangement as a strainer, through which it filters its microscopic food. At the merest suspicion of danger, quick as a flash, it folds, the entire "Christmas tree" into the tube.

POISON DART FROG

The poison dart frog is one of the loveliest creatures in the rainforests of South America. Maybe some of these creatures got together and agreed on who would take which color so that all the colors of the rainbow would be represented. One such frog is deep blue, another red with a green belly, while the bodies of others have spots of different colors. This rainbow-like beauty is not without purpose: it serves to warn animals thinking of eating the poison dart frog that it is extremely venomous. Some poison dart frogs eat ants. Others eat poisonous insects, without being poisoned themselves: they collect the poison in their skin, thereby making it into a kind of venomous armour. These poisons are so powerful that Native Americans used them to make poison darts. Other frogs with colorful skin only pretend to be poisonous. If you wish to avoid being eaten, the color trick comes in handy.

SPLENDID
BEAUTY

PANTHER
CHAMELEON

Who's been playing with the painting program? Or is this a particularly colorful piece of embroidery? Just wait until it moves and shoots out its long tongue as it snaps up a fly for its supper. This is a chameleon, and the keenest shades of red, blue, green, and yellow appear on its body without any help from computers or hardworking embroiderers. There is a plan behind the choice of colors—chameleons from different parts of the island of Madagascar opt for their own combination of colors as if they were wearing the jersey of a football club. Splendid colors are the province of the male chameleon. When two males meet, they show off to each other by changing colors and puffing themselves up. Less conspicuous brown females can only watch as the males compete for color supremacy.

WILSON'S BIRD-OF-PARADISE

Wilson's bird-of-paradise would be a worthy entrant in a competition for the title of World's Most Beautiful Bird. Let us seek it out in the tropical rainforests of Indonesia. If we're lucky, from our hiding place, we will see an extraordinary performance. The male bird-of-paradise will carefully clear a piece of ground, which he will use as a stage on which to dance and sing. He will show off the splendid colors of his feathers, the bright-blue skin on his head, and his long tail feathers, which are curved in impressive loops. What female could resist such a beautiful artist? Most performers attract several females at a time. As a bird-of-paradise mother must care for her eggs and young alone, she is of plain appearance, grey-brown in color—except for her blue head—to help her escape the attention of hungry beasts.

MANDARINFISH

No Eastern prince has ever worn a robe more magnificent than that of the mandarinfish. Just look at it, with its clear orange markings on a bright-blue background, its striped tail and fins, its light-green head, and its keen red eyes! Though barely as long as a finger, the mandarinfish proudly carries itself upright in its coral seascape as though walking on hind fins. With a slow, dignified gait, it patrols its small undersea kingdom meanwhile feeding on small invertebrates. Many aquarium keepers long to have this beauty in their collection, but few succeed in acquiring it—our proud piscine prince doesn't like to submit to a life in captivity.

MADAGASCAN SUNSET MOTH

Let's take a stroll together in the exotic forests of Madagascar. In the branches of a certain tree, we will notice some interesting-looking caterpillars. They are speckled black and white like the birch tree, and their head and legs are red. But what happens when the well-fed caterpillar pupates, and an adult butterfly flies out of the pupa? How magnificent the creature is then! The black-dappled wings dazzle us with every color we can imagine. This is because the delicate scales on the butterfly's wings reflect light. When these butterflies fly across Madagascar, a great many of them take to the air together. As their caterpillars are very picky about what they eat, adults are prepared to travel to the other side of the island to reach their favorite tree.

WATTLE CUP
CATERPILLAR

Extraterrestrials have landed on Earth and occupied northern Australia! Don't worry, that was a false alarm. But this caterpillar really does look as though it has flown in from another galaxy. Its angular body is covered in cosmic patterns of yellow, blue, orange ... And what about those weird antennae sticking out in all directions? Its appearance protects the Wattle Cup Caterpillar from enemies: many predators would think twice about eating such an odd-looking creature. And if some curious bird were to peck up this Australian caterpillar, it wouldn't easily forget doing so—the points on the caterpillar's antennae are poisonous and their sting more powerful than a wasp's. The adult butterfly isn't much to look at, however: it is as though it has forgotten all about its "youth."

CHAPTER
II.

Whew, so that would be it for the products of sheer madness. "Where was Mother Nature's head at?" someone might wonder. Hopefully, that little noodle of yours didn't get too dizzy. Many a spectator has left here with their necks so craned and contorted not even their parents recognized them. But now prepare for something more terryfing. Our next performance features creatures that have conquered death. They survived dinosaurs and the meteorite that brought ruin to the dinosaurs. They survived mammoths and the bitter ice age. Not even humans endangered them, and let me tell you, folks, they have destroyed quite a lot of things. The beings we're about to show you are the hardiest among the hardy, old-timers from an era not even your grandmothers and grandfathers or the grandmothers of your grandfathers and the grandfathers of your grandmothers experienced; remember, these are the oldest of the old, animals which have been around since time immemorial. Give a round of applause to our next performers, the living fossiiiiiiils!

LUNGFISH

If you wish to live on planet Earth for hundreds of millions of years, you must have special abilities. African lungfish have been masters of drought management since prehistoric times. They are happiest in shallow lakes that are nice and warm, but should their creek dry out, it wouldn't cross their mind to panic as other fish might. This is because they breathe not through gills but through special organs that work rather like our lungs. From their burrow in the mud, lungfish can wait for several years for proper rainfall to refill the lake. Neoceratodus forsteri, the Australian species of lungfish, may be envious of its African friends—it has only one lung, so it can go without water only for a few days.

TUATARA

Before the Mesozoic era, when Earth was ruled by dinosaurs, reptiles of the Sphenodontidae family were widespread. These reptiles are still with us today on several New Zealand islands. Although they look like large lizards, they differ from them in many respects and have characteristics we find in no other animals. Their mouths do not contain teeth but pointed growths from the jawbone that never fall out or decay. Stranger still, they have a third eye on top of their head. This isn't because the tuatara likes to keep an eye on what is going on above it head. However, as the creature becomes an adult, skin grows over this small eye. Tuatara do everything slowly—they move slowly, they digest slowly, they procreate slowly ... As they live for over 100 years, what's the hurry?

COELACANTH

The coelacanth didn't earn the title "living fossil" for nothing. For a long time, scientists knew of such fish with fins on muscular bodies only from fossils from the time of the dinosaurs. So when a live fish from this family was found off the coast of South Africa, it was a scientific sensation. The body of the coelacanth can be up to seven feet long, so it is no small fry. In appearance, it is probably like the fish that came ashore millions of years ago before gradually evolving into four-legged terrestrial animals. The coelacanth doesn't venture onto land, however; it is happy in the sea. It feeds on small marine animals and can swim on its back.

LIVING FOSSIL

HORSESHOE CRAB

In a competition for an animal to symbolize the Palaeozoic era, the trilobite would be a very strong contender. We see it often in fossilized form in museums. Although the sight of a live trilobite is something palaeontologists can only dream about, a cousin of the trilobite lives among us still. Called the horseshoe crab, it has barely changed in hundreds of millions of years. Covered in a hard shell with a long spine on its back, its body puts us in mind of an underwater tank moving slowly along the seabed. But this tank neither fires ammunition nor smashes into things. It doesn't move around on tracks but on several pairs of legs. If, by some misfortune, it loses a leg or two, there is no need for the services of a mechanic or a doctor for lost legs will grow back.

GOBLIN SHARK

At first sight, it appears that this shark escaped from a fairy-tale in which it was playing a wicked sprite. But it has swum to us from days long, long ago. Its distant ancestors may have even encountered ichthyosaurs in the oceans of the Mesozoic era. The special abilities of the goblin shark make it a pretty fabulous creature nonetheless. Deep in the sea, its long snout operates like an antenna, helping it track down fish or octopuses. When one swims by, the goblin shark shoots out its jaws and snaps up its prey. As it is not a very fast swimmer, it really needs this "ejector mouth" to save it from hunger.

CHAPTER III.

Sort of a walk around the haunted house, wouldn't you say? Natural zombies, one might think, right? Looking at you, though, I can see you're still not afraid. Unbelievable. Well, all right. Let's take a break from the scary stuff and try something completely different. Our next spectacle is so crazy you'll be laughing at me out of sheer disbelief. "You're pulling our legs!" your cries will resound in between the individual numbers. "You're a liar and talk nonsense. The stuff you're showing us can't possibly be real!" You'll boo me off the stage. And yet, it's real. The Magical Six that are getting ready to pounce on you might easily pass for someone completely different. They're masters of disguise, perfect doppelgängers. Get ready to receive animals that look like someone else!

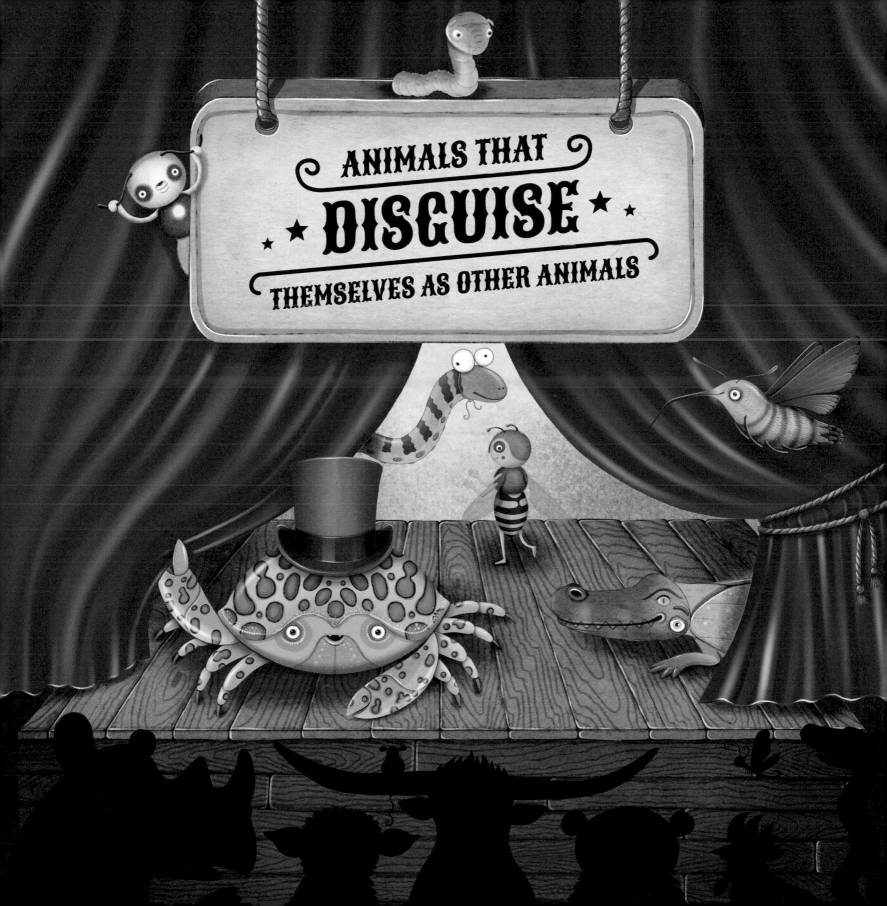

ANIMALS THAT DISGUISE

★ ★

★ ★

THEMSELVES AS OTHER ANIMALS

SYRPHUS RIBESII
HOVERFLY

No one sensible would choose to tangle with a wasp. It has sharp mandibles and a sting filled with venom, and it will brazenly attack anyone and everyone. As soon as its ominous yellow and black stripes appear, the best thing to do is get out of its way. The Syrphus ribesii hoverfly is aware of this, and it takes full advantage of this knowledge. To deter its enemies, it disguises itself as a wasp. Its striped abdomen looks truly dangerous, and no one thinks to count the wings: a wasp has four and this hoverfly only two. There is no risk of getting stung by a hoverfly. But aphids, which feed on plant juices, should be wary of it: the larvae of these stripy little creatures just love the taste of aphids!

PANDA ANT

What's that crawling over there? Although it has no wings and moves around the ground like an ant, we should be wary of it: it is a wasp with a really painful sting. So don't even dream of picking it up and cuddling it, though its hairy little body may tempt you to do so. The black and white spots on the body, which make it the spitting image of the famous giant panda, are a further attraction. Look at that white head and those black eyes! All it needs is some juicy bamboo to chew on! What the real panda thinks about this incredible resemblance we have yet to discover. As the giant panda lives in China and the panda ant lives in South America, it is unlikely they will ever meet.

23

HUMMINGBIRD HAWK-MOTH

Look, a hummingbird! It whirls its wings around flowers of the most beautiful colors and buries its beak in them. Could it have flown here all the way from a rainforest in South America? Of course not! This particular flower-lover is a butterfly, called the hummingbird hawk-moth. Its long proboscis can reach to the bottom of any flower, there to feast on its delicious sweet nectar. Its stout, hairy body and rather narrow wings truly do look like a bird's. Unlike other butterflies, the hummingbird hawk-moth doesn't sit on the flowers; instead, it flutters its wings and "hangs" in the air over them, just as a hummingbird does. This explains why many people believe that they have seen a hummingbird when they haven't (e.g., in a window box on a balcony or in a meadow).

UNBELIEVABLE DOPPELGÄNGER

25

MIMIC OCTOPUS

First prize in the Brilliant Disguise category goes to the mimic octopus by far. This octopus has up to fifteen different disguises in its repertoire! When in danger of being eaten by another creature, the mimic octopus can show itself as several different poisonous fishes, a sea serpent, and even a jellyfish—it chooses the disguise that will scare its hungry enemy the most. It performs these imitations by changing both color and body shape. It can puff itself up and twist in different directions, turning into a crab or a whelk for instance. When it wishes to be invisible, it makes itself look like a sea sponge, sand, or the stones on the seabed. How owners of fancy dress stores must envy the mimic octopus!

HEMEROPLANES
TRIPTOLEMUS MOTH

We find this expert in camouflage in the tropics of America. Although the adult Hemeroplanes triptolemus moth looks pretty innocent, its caterpillar can give you quite a scare. If you think it just sits calmly on a twig waiting for a hungry insectivore to come along and gobble it up, think again! It pushes out and puffs up the front part of its body, then thrusts its head at the enemy.

Looking just like a snake's, the head snaps at the attacker. Not even the hungriest predator will wait around for a sight of its jagged tongue and long, venomous teeth—so it doesn't get to see that the snake's head doesn't open and that legs grow out of the "forehead." This is no snake—it's a super-clever caterpillar.

CHAPTER IV.

I cannot believe you haven't gone crazy yet. Not even this bunch managed to twist your mind? Well, hats off to you, I suppose. What a tough gang of small daredevils you turned out to be. You might consider joining us. Think about it. "And now, a group of the toughest children in the world!" What a hit. Though your parents are probably waiting for you at home, dinner ready and everything, huh? I bet your mouths started watering and tummies started growling the moment I mentioned it, didn't they? But what we arranged now will drive all those thoughts away, trust me. That's because our next performers suffer from quite a bizarre appetite. If you did in your school cafeteria what these maniacs do on a daily basis, your moms and dads would be pretty shocked by the little freaks they raised. Then you'd really have no other choice but join us. But what's that sound? Our animals with unusual eating habits are already storming the stage. And I'm off so that they don't gobble me up by accident . . .

ANIMALS THAT GET
THEIR FOOD
IN A SPECIAL WAY

SMOOTH-HEAD BLOBFISH

Is this truly a fish? It looks more like a pile of jelly with a big, bobbly nose! The blobfish collapses into a pile only when pulled from the water in a net, however, at home in the sea, it is shaped like most other fish. As it evolved, the blobfish lost all its bones and muscles, turning into a gelatinous substance to better resist the immense water pressure—it lives at depths of up to almost one mile. Without bones and muscles, it can't swim fast enough to catch much to eat, but this is not a problem. It is not picky about its food and is satisfied with particles of food that fall to the seabed from higher in the ocean, finding these right under its nose!

ELEPHANTNOSE FISH

Small eyes, a large brain, and a trunk-like growth on its lower lip. If, like the elephantnose fish (for this is our creature), you lived in muddy African rivers and hunted food at night, when you couldn't see your own fin, you would appreciate a good flashlight. The elephantnose fish has a rather technically sophisticated hunting kit. From a strange organ near its tail, it sends out a weak electric field, which bounces off everything in its vicinity. The "trunk" on its lip is actually an antenna, which receives the signals that come back and sends them to the brain. An amazing processing unit, the brain, swiftly figures out what lies within the hungry fish's reach. A pebble? A root? No, thanks. A mosquito larva buried in the mud? Yum, yum, I'll have that!

THORNY DEVIL

This Australian lizard is one of the weirdest creatures on our planet. Its body is covered with terrible-looking spines; the top of its head supports another, false "head," which distracts enemies on the attack, can change color, and so on. The thorny devil's diet is dull in the extreme: ants, ants, and more ants. Sounds less than juicy, doesn't it? A diet of ants should be washed down well. But where can you get water in the Australian desert? The thorny devil has found an answer to that: its skin works like blotting paper or a sponge. Its fine pores take water from sand damp with morning dew; it sometimes buries its legs in the sand to make this easier. The water then passes through the skin to the mouth, where it is swallowed. Cheers!

LIZARD
FROM HELL

33

ALLIGATOR SNAPPING TURTLE

This North American cayman is a real hefty eater among turtles. It will eat whatever it finds, as long as the catch has flesh on it: fish, snails, frogs, snakes, crayfish, worms, other turtles, ducks and other aquatic birds, and even mice, coypus, and small alligators. As it hunts mostly at night, to not get hungry in daytime, it relies on a tactic that is also a favorite with fishermen. What's the best bait for catching a fish? A nice fat worm, of course. And here's a juicy one, thrashing around! But as soon as the fish reaches for the "worm," the cayman's jaws snap shut. That was no worm, but the cayman's tongue, which wags around in the turtle's open mouth to lure the fish into its trap.

AYE-AYE

We find the arboreal animal called the aye-aye only in Madagascar. Including its tail, it is around three feet in length—no small fry. And a sizeable body needs ample helpings of food. The aye-aye didn't have to read books on nutrition to learn that insects are the best source of protein around. The search for its favorite food provides it with a full-time occupation. It roams the branches and taps on the bark with its fingers, listening for the sound of larvae drilling in the wood. As soon as it detects a grub, it gnaws a hole in the bark, into which it pokes its long middle finger before elegantly scooping out its lunch. In the same way, it picks out delicious coconut flesh and bamboo pulp. Protein is protein, but lunch should be rounded off with something sweet.

35

MYRMELEON

On meeting an adult Myrmeleon, which looks like a cross between a mosquito and a dragonfly, it would never occur to you that its child looks like this. That's right, this is the younger Myrmeleon! With its mouth open wide, its menacing mandibles have but one task—to snap up its favorite food, ants. But as the Myrmeleon is too cumbersome to pursue its prey, it has developed a unique hunting technique. It finds a nice, dry, sandy spot, where it digs a funnel-shaped hole; then, it hides in the hole and waits. The moment an ant comes crawling by, the Myrmeleon begins to throw sand at it, stopping only when it succeeds in knocking the ant down into the hole. This is the perfect trap: the ant has no chance of escape and the Myrmeleon gets its snack.

VELVET WORM

Although it looks like a mix between a slug and a centipede, it is actually a completely unrelated, very old group of invertebrates. It lives in hot regions of the southern hemisphere, enjoys a carnivore's diet, and goes hunting at night. It preys on termites, spiders, and gastropods as large as itself. At first, the velvet worm creeps up on its prey without making a sound. As the worm feels its prey with its antennae, it asks itself, "Will this taste good? Is it worth it?" If it decides that it is, it shoots from its mouth a sticky liquid that solidifies on contact with air; in an instant, the prey is completely immobilized. A gathering of velvet worms can share in a single catch. After its meal, the velvet worm will crawl away to digest at its leisure—it goes hunting only once every few weeks.

CHAPTER

V.

I can see you facepalm in sheer disbelief. Yes, dearies, that indeed was real and no dream, no doubt about it. Yes, you are up and in full possession of your senses, though I'd recommend easing up on that facepalming; not exactly fun, having a bump on your head. But even if you managed to get one already, do not despair! Compared to what our next performers have growing on their heads, and not only there, a bump is nothing at all. Get ready for limbs that grow out of places nothing should ever grow. Some of these animals might remind you of horny devils; others should drop by a good hairdresser or dentist, pronto. I don't want to reveal more than strictly necessary, though I do need to warn you well in advance that wouldn't do anyone any good if we ended up having to revive you, gentle folks. But for the moment, long live animals with growths they should have never had.

PACU FISH

The pacu comes from South America. Like people, however, today's fish travel with the times and can be found all over the world. Aquarists in countries such as the USA and Sweden have released this overgrown aquarium fish into the wild. Imagine the expression of incredulity on a Swedish fisherman's face when this three-foot-long creature bares its human-like teeth at him from the water! This is neither a joke nor a crazy scientific experiment. The pacu is a relative of the piranha. But unlike the piranha, its teeth are not sharp and shark-like but square, looking very much like a human's. At home in Amazonia, it uses these "grinders" to chew nuts, which it feeds on. This fish may be a vegetarian, but we advise you not to put your finger in its mouth.

EMEI MOUSTACHE TOAD

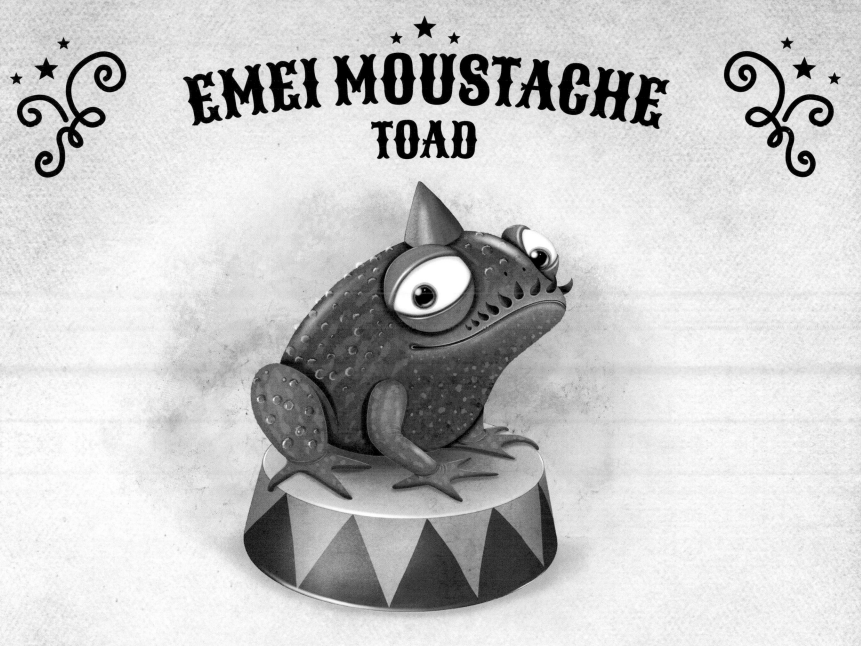

As the Three Musketeers knew many years ago, the moustache can be a fine addition to the male face. The Emei moustache toad shares this knowledge. Although the male of this toad can take pride in his lovely purple color all year round, when the breeding season comes around, he must find something new to dazzle the ladies. So he lets hard, pointed spines grow on his upper lip. These spines look rather like carefully sharpened crayons. But there will be no crayoning here: these spines are to go into battle with. While a musketeer would draw his rapier to fight for a lady's honor, the Emei moustache toad faces his rivals with his moustache to the fore. Those who fail to get out of the way can get a nasty prick. Maybe the nickname "cactus toad" would be more suitable than "moustache toad."

41

HORNED TARANTULA

LEGGY DEVIL

Tarantulas, brothers of spiders, are big and hairy. They have eight legs ... and sometimes a horn too. That's right, a horn! In Africa, there is a whole family of horned tarantulas that have this strange growth on their back, making them look like a spider-rhinoceros cross. This hitherto unknown species was discovered in Angola not so long ago. Its horn is much longer than that of its horned relatives. This horn is tub-shaped, soft, and made of fatty tissue, so we might argue that the creature looks more like a spider-camel cross. And some scientists really do believe that this unusual addition to the back serves for the storing of supplies, much like a camel's hump. Unlike it, however, the tarantula's hump doesn't take on passengers. The tarantula is a proud, venomous creature.

43

SPIDER-TAILED HORNED VIPER

One of several horned vipers, the raised scales above the eyes of this snake from the rocky landscapes of Iran give it the appearance of a devil or a dragon. However, it has a far more interesting growth at the other end of its body: attached to the tip of its tail is something that looks like a live spider! With its swollen abdomen and legs shooting out in all directions, you would think it was used to deter enemies. But this spider lookalike serves not as a defense but as a lure. Some birds have no fear of venomous spiders; indeed, they like to eat them. But when they take a peck at this rather chubby spider, the snake's head leaps out from its hiding place and makes a meal out of the poor tricked bird.

YETI CRAB

It may have a monkey's coat, but it certainly isn't a monkey. Meet the Kiwa crab, the owner of the longest hair in the ocean realm. Underwater, the sight of such hairy legs is a rare one indeed! The first time researchers saw these crabs, they were reminded of the Yeti, otherwise known as the abominable snowman. The coat comes in handy in the winter; at other times, however, this crab doesn't have much need of it as it lives near the ocean bed, where warm water is discharged. The hair serves the crab more as a private garden than a coat. Between the fibers, it grows bacteria, which it combs out using the brushes on its claws and then eats. Imagine something like bilberries growing in your hair, ready for you to gather whenever you felt peckish!

CHAPTER VI.

I hope you are not exhausted and your eyes still work as they should, because I'm going to show you something you've never seen before. The creatures we're about to encounter live in pitch dark in deep, dark ocean waters or right in the heart of exotic jungles, where they lie in wait for clueless prey they can lure with their little lights. The innocent victims often don't even realize that the enticing light is the last one they'll ever going to see the light at the end of the tunnel, so to speak. And the animals that don't use their tiny lamps in the fine art of dinner-catching use them instead to frighten their enemies or sticky-fingered snoops. On the other hand, one of our rising stars uses her gifts to enchant a partner who, deceived by her gentle light, falls in love at first sight. So beware of any light—small and large—you notice glowing in the dark. If you're not careful, you might lose your heart or worse, become someone else's "what's for for dinner ..."

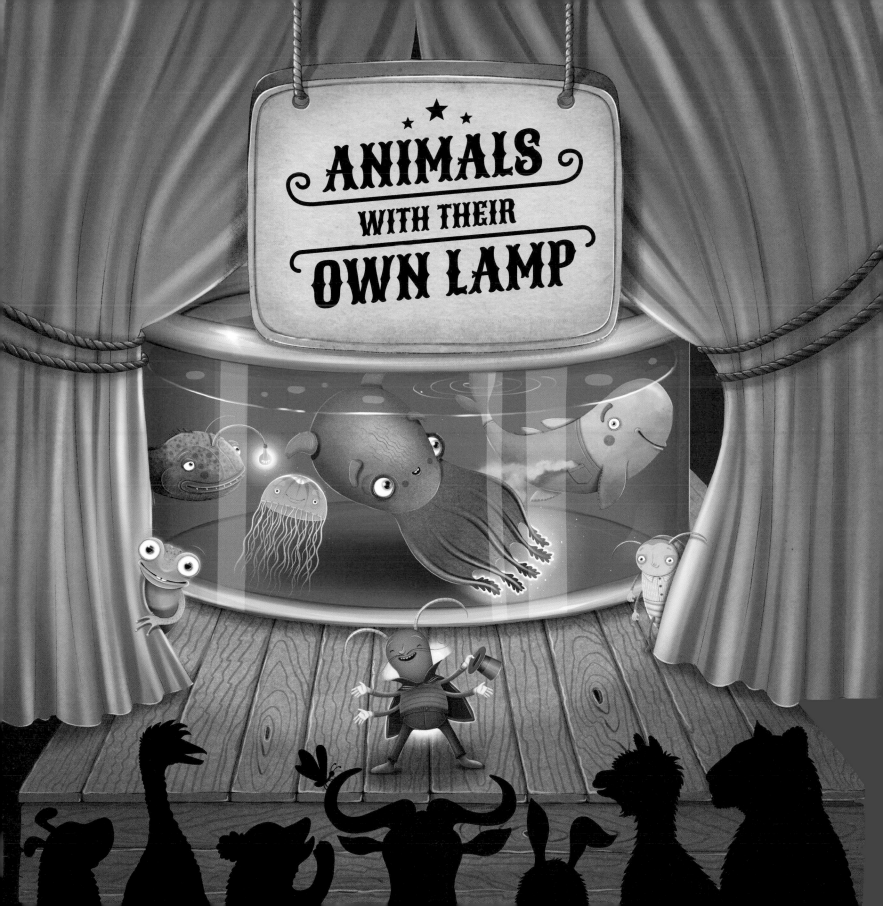

ANIMALS
WITH THEIR
OWN LAMP

VAMPIRE SQUID

Light coming from the deep! This is the work of the vampire squid, a small sea creature related to the octopus. It gets its name from its red eyes and its webbing, which looks like a bat's wing or Count Dracula's cloak. It has nothing in common with the vampire, however: this squid feeds on dead creatures that have sunk to the bottom of shallow ocean waters. Most of the vampire squid's body is covered with organs filled with luminescent bacteria, which can produce a continuous or flashing light as well as dim the light or increase its intensity. The light show serves a vital purpose: it surprises and scares away fish and other marine hunters who would like to eat this little monster.

48

CRYSTAL JELLY

It floats around in the northern parts of the Pacific Ocean. Its transparent, luminescent body looks rather like a chandelier. Like all jellyfish, the crystal jelly drags in its wake long stinging tentacles, which it uses to immobilize small sea creatures. As it doesn't harm humans, divers can enjoy its luminous splendour without fear. The crystal jelly's blue-green light is produced by chemical reactions between several substances in its body. Scientists borrowed one of these compounds for use as a fluorescent marker in experiments with cells and genes, so discovering a method that earned them a Nobel Prize. The crystal jelly has reason to be proud!

ANGLERFISH

Have you ever seen such a flat fish before? It looks like someone has stepped on the anglerfish. This is because it lives at the bottom of the ocean, up to 3000 feet deep, and its flatness helps it survive the immense pressure of the water. As no light reaches such a depth, the anglerfish makes its own: its "lantern" hangs on the end of one of three filaments that grow from its back. By means of a chemical reaction, this special organ emits blue light. Does it help its owner to see its way? Hardly! In fact, it works as an ingenious bait, encouraging smaller fish to come closer before the anglerfish snatches them up at lightning speed with their mouth filled with pointed teeth.

AMERICAN POCKET SHARK

In 2010, US scientists discovered a new species of shark in the Gulf of Mexico. But don't imagine a dorsal fin and menacing jaws breaking the surface; this shark, whose head looks like that of a small whale, represents no danger to divers or swimmers. And as it is only about as long as the human hand, it would easily fit in your pocket. However, it is called a "pocket shark" because of the pockets on its body, close to the gills. As it moves around in the sea at a relatively great depth, these pockets release a luminous fluid that floats, attracting the attention of small fish. The shark then makes an easy catch by attacking its unsuspecting prey from below.

HEADLIGHT ELATER

The rainforests of South and Central America have many strange inhabitants. One of these emits such a powerful light that it is said to be strong enough to read by. The Headlight Elater always carries three lamps: two on the side segments above the wing cases and the third is a broad area on the abdomen. These organs emit light by means of the same chemical reaction as in fireflies. The Headlight Elater can also increase the intensity of its light—when it needs to drive away an enemy, it shines a fierce light in its eyes. Not only do the adult beetles emit light, but the larvae and even the eggs do too. No surprise, then, that this creature has earned the title World's Most Luminous Beetle.

CHAPTER VII.

We're nearing the end slowly but surely. It is true, my friends. I, too, am getting teary-eyed just thinking about it. But alas, such is life. Everything good must come to an end sooner or later. In our case, everything crazy, that is. And if you don't like it and feel like making me continue, remember I have a team of the best defenders at my disposal. Sort of bodyguards, one might say. But they're not just some regular soccer or hockey-players. These are the ultimate masters of self-defense. Karate? Judo? Taekwondo? Pah! You know where you can stick those. The tricks known to this group are a mystery for everyone: spines, armour, swords, venom ... and that's only a fraction of what we're going to show you. So be very, very careful! Our tiny stage might just about turn into a veritable arena where gladiators fight to the death. Please welcome our last performers and prepare yourselves because the masters of self-defense are coming!

COMMON CUTTLEFISH

The cuttlefish is the favorite prey of many large sea creatures, including octopuses, sharks, and dolphins. No wonder, then, that it has mastered various strategies to protect itself from being eaten. The best of these ensure that the hunter fails to spot the cuttlefish altogether. To blend in with its surroundings, the cuttlefish can change color at will. It can also make itself "invisible" to the electric sense of sharks by going stiff and covering the openings of its gills with its tentacles. In this way, it reduces the electric field around its body to such a degree that the shark's "radar" doesn't pick it up. When camouflage doesn't work, the cuttlefish turns to other tricks, such as spraying its predator with a gush of water or ink, covering its retreat.

SUNDA SLOW LORIS

Danger! Looking at the Sunda slow loris, you wouldn't think it was poisonous, would you? This cute furry thing is a relative of the monkey. Its wide, staring eyes and slow swings from branch to branch give it a pretty defenseless appearance. And it's true that it can't run away from its enemies; instead, it resists them with an excretion produced on the insides of its elbows. This venomous substance takes effect on contact with saliva. The mixture is spread all over the loris's body as it licks itself and combs its fur with its teeth. A dutiful loris mother cares for her young in the same way, so allowing her to leave them for a while without supervision. No eagle or snake, no matter how hungry, will feast on a poisonous loris.

SOUTHERN THREE-BANDED ARMADILLO

At first sight, the armadillo looks rather like a species of extinct lizard, but in fact, it is a mammal. When it got itself a handsome shell, perhaps it was inspired by turtle fashion. This shell is made of the same material as human nails, and its plates overlap each other so tightly that they leave no gap. You might expect this armour to offer perfect protection, but unfortunately, it has a weak point: as it covers the back only, by turning the armadillo over, the enemy can strike at its belly. But the South American three-banded armadillo stays a step ahead of its foes. As soon as it senses danger, it rolls into a ball—as if about to perform a somersault—packing all the soft parts of its body inside its armor and leaving nothing for the enemy to attack.

MIND-BLOWING
TRANSFORMATION

FLYING FISH

What a maddening experience it is for a hunter when his prey flies away from right in front of him! And if that prey is a fish, it's even more maddening! Flying fish are masters of this strategy, not least as their pectoral fins are shaped very much like bird wings. They may not be able to flap these "wings", although they do allow the flying fish to glide like an airplane. Although only about 8-inches long, it can jump up to 20 feet above the surface of the water at a speed of 44 miles per hour—which is about twice as fast as the human record sprinter. And that's not all that flying fish can do: with great skill, they bounce off the waves, which allows them to land far from the starting point and change direction in midair.

HAGFISH

Although it looks like an eel, it isn't really a fish. It would be truer to say that the hagfish is a distant cousin of the fish, which has barely changed in its hundreds of millions of years of ocean life. And why should it? Quite literally, it slips away from its enemies. The glands on its body secrete a great deal of slime, which expands in water. This makes catching a hagfish about as easy as catching a snake coated with a thick layer of custard. And if anyone tries to do so, the hagfish has another trick up its sleeve: it ties a knot in its serpentine body, pushes it from its head to its tail, and shoots all its slime directly at its attacker. Most hungry creatures of the seas have learned their lesson and stay well away from the hagfish.

BOMBARDIER
BEETLE

Have you ever heard of insect artillery? The bombardier beetle is a small beetle that runs fast and has shiny, metallic-green wing cases. As it hunts other insects, it must take care not to be hunted and killed itself. In self-defense, it uses a weapon of very high calibre. Its abdomen acts a bit like a cannonball, although it doesn't use gunpowder to fire cannons but releases doses of a certain chemical compound. It produces this substance continuously, storing it in containers in its abdomen. Not only is the stinking mixture it sprays at its enemy boiling hot, but it also has the force of a shot. The enemy has to hurry to get out of the bombardier's range. Builders of aircraft engines are very interested in the bombardier, as they would love to imitate the beetle's technology.

LONG-SPINE PORCUPINEFISH

Meet the long-spine porcupinefish, a charmingly spotted inhabitant of tropical seas and oceans the world over. Looks good, doesn't it? If you get on well with it, you will find it a nice chap with an ordinary fish-like appearance. But you should see it when it gets angry! Which is just what happens when someone tries to eat it. It puffs itself up into a ball—an act that is enough to scare the enemy away. On top of this, however, it bristles the spines on its porcupine-like body (at rest, these flow backwards). A prickly ball is not an appetizing prospect. What's more, the long-spine porcupinefish is venomous. Any would-be predator is well advised to find something less dangerous for lunch or as an enemy to attack.

INDEX

albatros
www.albatrosbooks.com

Author: Jana Nová. Illustrator: Zuzana Dreadka Krutá.
© Designed by B4U Publishing for Albatros, an imprint of Albatros Media Group, 2021. Na Pankráci 30, Prague 4, Czech Republic.
Printed in Ukraine by Unisoft.